Violet Flint

A Golfing Idyll

Or, the Skipper's Round with the Deil on the Links of St. Andrews

Violet Flint

A Golfing Idyll
Or, the Skipper's Round with the Deil on the Links of St. Andrews

ISBN/EAN: 9783337190538

Printed in Europe, USA, Canada, Australia, Japan

Cover: Foto ©Andreas Hilbeck / pixelio.de

More available books at **www.hansebooks.com**

A Golfing Idyll

OR

The Skipper's Round with the Deil

On the Links of St Andrews

Third Edition

W. C. HENDERSON & SON, ST ANDREWS
GEO. STEWART & CO., EDINBURGH AND LONDON
SIMPKIN, MARSHALL, KENT & CO. LD., LONDON

MDCCCXCVII.

PREFACE

As some prefatory explanation may reasonably be expected as to how I became acquainted with the subject of the following narrative,—'A Golfing Idyll,' I have had the presumption to call it,—I may inform the reader that circumstances induced me, a lady medical student, at present studying in London, to take my Autumn holiday in St Andrews. I know the old place well, and have many acquaintances there. As to Golf I can, I think, hold my own with most of the Golfing sisterhood, and am well up in the jargon of the Links and game. One day found me, sketch-book in hand, sitting on the brae-side by the butts, behind the Club. As I sat, listlessly toying with my pencil, and quietly enjoying the scene before me, I remarked a man, whom I had not previously observed, also sitting, a few yards off, on the slope towards the sea. On closer inspection I recognised him to be an old Caddie, well known to most frequenters of the Links, but not very creditably, I am sorry to say, as he was one of the sad victims of the vice that has cut off so many poor fellows of his class. I noticed at the same time that he now looked very decent and respectable, was neatly

dressed in blue serge, a bit of blue ribbon apparent
on the lapel of his coat, and that altogether he had
the appearance of a person well cared for. He
seemed to be engaged in an agreeable conversation
with himself. As he sat, smiling and muttering, he
was shortly joined by another man, a stranger to
me, a ruddy-faced jolly-looking personage, with a
free and easy manner, who proved also to be a
Caddie. As to how the latter accosted his old
friend, and what followed, is all described in the
' Idyll.'

As I was only a few yards distant from them, I
could hear distinctly every word they uttered. The
old man did not seem to mind my presence in the
least. Before commencing his tale he looked round,
saw me, and, with a back toss of his head which
seemed to say to his friend, ' Oh, it is only a lassie,'
proceeded with his story. Throughout the narrative
he was exceedingly animated—rising, sitting down,
and gesticulating, as if under the influence of con-
siderable excitement and emotion, evidently earnestly
intent on impressing on the listener the truth of what
he was relating. The latter listened open-eyed and
open-mouthed, uttering occasional ejaculations, such
as, Oh Lord! Gude sake! Ay man! etc.

The Skipper delivered himself of what he had to say in pure Scotch Doric, more or less, but occasionally broke out into good English, showing himself to be a man of better education than I believed him to be. This idea was strengthened by his reference to Bunyan; and the extravagant vision at the 'end hole,' with all its bathos and absurdity, suggested some acquaintance with Milton.

I listened most attentively. I have a good memory, and when I got home I committed to paper all that I remembered, most carefully. Moreover, I had several interviews with the old gentleman, and have done my best to convey to the reader, as accurately as I could, his version of his extraordinary adventure.

As to my reason for weaving the story into rhyming doggerel, I hold myself excused in that I did it for my own amusement, influenced also by a belief that it might possibly prove more readable and attractive in that shape to the persons I chiefly wished to peruse it, viz., my friends of the Caddie fraternity.

VIOLET FLINT.

TORRINGTON MANSIONS,
LONDON.

PREFACE TO THIRD EDITION

Since I penned the first prefatory lines to this trifling work, I regret to inform my readers non-resident in St Andrews, that my interesting old friend the Skipper is no more. He died at the ripe age of 75. Peace to his memory! Some time before his death, I had what proved to be a final interview with him, when he rehearsed his queer weird story, adding some curious reminiscences of his early days in connection with the Links of St Andrews and his favourite pastime. As they may be interesting to some of my older golfing friends, I have inter-polated them into the rugged doggerel of the text from the notes I took at the time. He also at the same time pathetically deplored the unreasoning and obstinate incredulity of friends who persisted in disbelieving his story, and suggested, with a view to convincing and converting them, that I should have some of the more striking incidents in the story illustrated. I have done so, but alas! his old eyes will never look upon them and acknowledge the credit due to Mr Bannerman, the clever draughtsman.

B

At the close of our interview, he also alluded to his precious breeks with which, in his opinion, rest the *onus probandi* of his adventure. It was his intention, he told me, to have them framed and glazed, with the fateful mark prominently displayed— the date, incident, etc., carefully printed—to be made over at his death to the local Museum, and safe custody of Mr Couttes. It was not every man, he proudly asserted, who could receive and survive a skelp o' the Deil's tail!

V. F.

TORRINGTON MANSIONS,
LONDON.

A GOLFING IDYLL

Now Skipper frien', come tell me true
What garred ye mount the ribbon blue?
Gude sake! to think the like o' you
Should e'er hae joined the Templar crew!
How you accomplished your conversion
It bangs poor me past comprehension.
No six months gane, a drucken deevil,
You led the ball in waste and revel;
Were staggerin' on destruction's brink,
Selling your very duds for drink.
Now, there you sit, you grim auld sinner,
And tell's the smell o't mak's you scunner,
As mim as howdie at a christening,
Or tinker to a sermon listening;
Weel washed, weel clad, your blue beard shaved
Like Dr Byd's, and weel behaved
As toun-kirk elder 'fore the session—
Speak out, auld man, and mak' confession.

The speaker was ane Jock Pitbladdie,
A golfer good, and decent caddie,
Who, drunk or sober, in's vocation

Had aye the grace o' moderation.
A souter to his trade, he'd left the toun
Sax months before to work in Troon,
To carry clubs or mend auld shoon,
At ilka trade a handy loon.
Skipper and Jock were cronies thrang,
Had kent and liked each other lang ;
Mony a gill they'd drunk thegither,
And friendly treated ane anither.
Jockie was like a bed of sand,
The more he drank, the more he'd stand ;
But Skipper, wud, and wilder grew,
And never stopped till roarin' fou.
What wonder, then, at Jock's surprise
To find his frien' in siclike guise,
Or Jock's ill-mannered exclamation
And rough demand for explanation.

The Skipper lookit sair offended,
And muttering growled, his hand extended.—
Queer manners you hae brocht frae Troon ;
Come here, you jawing gowk, sit doon.
Instead of coorse and ill reflections
On my past life, and ways, and actions,
Your greetin' might hae been more ceevil,
You ill-condeetioned gabbin' deevil.

A GOLFING IDYLL.

Hoot, Skipper, nae offence was meant,
For you and I are weel acquaint.
Now dicht your mou', and tell me true
How cam' ye by that bit o' blue?

The Skipper gazed as wise and solemn
As if he felt his hand on helm
His cutter o'er the green waves guiding,
Close hauled, through kittle channel gliding.
Oh, Jock! I doot I'm rash to tell ye
What strange and awfu' things befell me,
Unless like me you'd warning tak',
Ere sorrow lay you on your back.
Sae, to avert sic dismal fate,
My woful tale I'll now relate.—
He sighed and spat, then sighed again,
And thus his simple tale began :

'Twas on a summer's afternoon,
Just after you had gane to Troon,
I foregather'd wi' ane Tammas Trail,
Auld mate o' mine who bides in Crail.
A man o' means, wi' nets and boat,
A fisher keen, and much afloat ;
A very decent chappie Tam,
Who, like me, dearly lo'ed his dram.

He kent my weakness, nocht would serve him,
But I maun tak' my supper wi' him.
The supper was baith het and good—
No that I'm nice about my food ;
We'd rizzared haddies, if you please,
Tripe and ingans, toasted cheese,
And whiskey grand frae Cameron Brig,
Better was never 'stilled by Haig.
And, oh ! a jolly time we had,
For my pairt I was skirlin' mad,
And Tammie, he was in his glory,
Just ripplin' o'er wi' joke and story.
But a' things good maun hae an end,
Baith joys and pains o' human kind,
And Time, the thief, wi' spitefu' stroke,
Snecket our fun 'fore ten o'clock—
That nicht—the thocht o't gars me grue,
Ahint the joy there cam' sic rue.

Now, Jocky, I must here explain
I wasna drunk, just fou ye ken ;
Just fresh and free and swaggerin' canty,
And bauld as Wallace wight and vaunty.
My hairt was licht, my feet were dancin'
Like struttin' cock, or stallion prancin'.
Bethought me, as I steered alang,

I'll get my clubs, to the Links I'll gang.
Should a' the folk to roost hae gane,
I car'd na if I played alane.
The nicht was fine, the moon was shinin',
The time between the mirk and gloamin';
As far as I could view the green,
No living soul could there be seen.

Nigh the brig I drove a bonny shot,
My second was the marrow o't,
The third gaed in—I holed in three,
As proud as Punch, I skirled wi' glee;
And swaggerin' fou, and fit and fettle,
Was wild to back my skill and mettle;
And, madlike, shouted out aloud,
You might hae heard me doon the road,
'Od! I'd play the very Deil himsel',
Auld Nickey Ben, red wud frae H—l.'
I heard a laugh! Was I mistaen?
I thocht I was my lief alane,
But turnin', near me stood a man,
A strappin' chiel, wi' clubs in han',—
Lean-shankit, extra tall and spare,
Wi' goatee beard and jet-black hair.
'Good evening, Skipper,' says he sprightly,
Liftin' his cap to me politely.

'You want a match, I'll gladly play you
For a hundred pounds, what say you?'
'You do me proud,' says I, astounded,
My wits had left me quite confounded.
'Man, a hundred pounds, I hae nae got,
I'm but a Caddie, poor my lot;
To play you I am proud and willin',
But I ne'er gang beyond a shillin'.'
'Oh, d—m your shilling!' says he so fine,
'Why, don't you see, your sure to win—
You are a strong, well-known professional,
And play a game that's quite sensational;
While my performance is but poor,
That of a first-class amateur.
But player good, I stand confessed,
Who plays 'gainst me must play his best.
But if you're shy, why odds I'll give you,
A stroke a hole, will that not tempt you?
And should I have the luck to win
(He said this with a leering grin),
Why what so simple, you engage
To serve me faithful without wage,
And as my Caddie with me stay
Until your little debt you pay.
Service with me will never tire you,
Besides I like you and admire you.'

Softly he spoke, while sweetly smilin'
Like lover simple lass beguilin';
Then from his pooch a purse he pulled,
A purse with golden guineas filled;
The meshes thro' I saw them bright
Glitterin' in the gloamin' light.
'Look, Skipper see these yellow boys,
The source and fount of human joys;
With them you grasp the dear delights
Of festive days and glorious nights.'

Dazed, dazzled, fou, and half-demented,
Oh, Jocky! I was sairly tempted.
No wonder that I soon consented,
And muckle less that I repented.
But to my tale—'All right,' says I,
'A bargain be it, I comply;
A stroke a hole—I tak' your offer,
Altho' you treat me like a duffer.'
For troth I felt no little nettled
To find my good game so belittled.

But, Skipper, you have yet to tell
What he was like, this bloomin' swell.

I said he was a strappin' chiel,

Six feet and mair frae head to heel ;
On's head he wore a Hieland bannet,
A blackcock's feather stickin' in it.
On either side his lugs I noted
Were large and high and sharply nookit ;
A nose like mine, and fine black een,
A big moustache and pointed chin ;
In troth a very handsome felley,
Though black-a-vized and somewhat yelley,
Like they foreign chaps that gang wi' puggies,
And play on pipes and hurdy-gurdies.
His dress was black, good velveteen,
His stockin's red and cravit green,
And on his feet were yellow boots,—
I little dreamed they covered cloots !
I kent na wha I was to play wi',
The truth it never dawned upon me ;
I thocht he was some Glasgow billy,
Or chap frae Sooth, Golf-mad and silly,
Wi' little wit and siller plenty,
The country's rife wi' sic like gentry.

'And what's your honour's name,' quoth I ?
I felt no whit abashed or shy—
'My name is Dr Nicholas Ben Clootie,
Hades my home, a place of radiant beauty ;

A region warm, perhaps a trifle sooty,
Still an alluring and delicious place is Hades,
Frequented much by lords and ladies.
So charming and so pleasant is it
That multitudes to Paradise prefer it.'
' Hades, ne'er heard o't, is't in the Hielands ? '
' No, Skipper friend, 'tis in the Netherlands.'
' But come, our game, I'm eager to begin ;
Strike off,' said I, ' I long those yellow boys to win.
Tak' you the honour noo, for ne'er again
You'll hae the chance, or I'm sair mistaen.'
He grinned, and said, ' You hold me very cheap ;
Believe me, I intend those yellow boys to keep.'

He drove a rattlin' shot from off the tee ;
I followed with as good, as far as he.
Our next we dropped upon the green.
Twa bonny strokes as e'er were seen.
Stane dead I lay, he ten feet aff,
He missed his putt—wi' careless laugh,
' First blood,' cried I, ' the hole is mine.'
' Yes,' quo' he, ' the Devil's luck is thine.'

So cocky was I with this fine beginnin',
I offered straight to play him even.
' No, no,' he said, ' to that I can't agree,

You'll need your odds before you've done wi' me.'
He looked and said this with a wicked leer,
I felt my flesh to creep with sudden fear.
Such confidence and pluck, I could not understand,
And funkit something strange, uncanny, underhand.

But spite of funk and fancy, all the same
I played weel up a rattlin' game ;
Holes three and four they fell to me,
The taen at four, the tither at three.
His Highness meanwhile skipped alang,
Whiles he whistled and whiles he sang ;
But whenever I turned, his leerin' e'e
Was glarin', glowerin', lookin' at me !

At ' Hole Across,' the bunker of H—l,
To my surprise he kent it well ;
He girned and cackled and looked excited
As if wi' secret thoughts delighted.
I drove weel o'er, wi' grand precision,
And lay serene on sod Elysian.
Clootie on purpose missed his ba',
And landed slap intil its maw.
Then, Jock, a sicht I saw, so strange and awfie,
Unseen, unheard o', and unlawfie !
Loud laughter rose from H—l within,

Wild shouts and cries o' welcomin' ;
While over the edge, peepin' and peerin'
Through the long grass, and disappearin',
Were seen strange forms, like horned apes,
And other brutes wi' fearsome shapes,
Goblins grinning wi' blazing een.
Bogles or ghaists, or a cross between.
But strange, when we the bunker neared,
They'd vanished all and disappeared.
And nocht remained but an infernal smell
Of brimstone reek, true stink o' H—l.
Clootie gaed smilin' in, rejoiced to be
At hame, his bonny bairns to see ;
His ball he found, both safe and playable.
' Play quick,' cried I, ' this smell is d—able.'
' Pause, Skipper, 'tis my favourite scent,' says he,
' Bouquet d'Enfer, a perfume sweet to me.
You lack good taste, you drunken sot,
To me this is a charming spot ;
But play I must,' and, as he spoke,
He drove forthwith a splendid stroke ;
But of little good it proved to be,
For again I took the hole in three.

' Four up,' I said, ' my gallant foe ;
If this goes on you'll come to woe.'

'All right,' says he, ' my chance will come,
I'll show you play when we turn home.
To see your game was such a treat,
Great was my luck with you to meet ;
You are indeed a beauty without paint,
The picture of a drouthy saint.'
And thus he sneered and scoffed and chaffed,
While at my speech he mocked and laughed;
From fearing I began to hate him,
And vow'd I'd do my best to beat him.
But man is frail, and human vows
Aye come to nocht, when they oppose
The powers that rule for good or evil,
And my opponent was the Deevil.
Blind, stupid, and wi' drink demented,
I couldna see nor comprehend it ;
But soon, alas! I learned the truth,
Wi' mental pain and muckle ruth.

The moon still shed its blessed light
And calm and lovely was the night.
Oh, Daavid! had you but been there,
Wi' your leemonade and your ginger-beer,
You might have saved me from despair,
And a' the horrors that befell me,
Which, Jockie, I am now to tell ye.

My game, I told you had been good,
Nine holes to play, eight up I stood.
Sick o' the game, and sicker far o' Clootie,
I'd ceased to care about the booty.
I thocht I'd bounce him wi' my swagger,
And get the better o' the beggar.
' Doctor,' says I ' I've licked you into fits,
Throw up the sponge, play double or quits!'
' What!' shouted he, 'such cheek, you sot,
Dost think me daft, you silly Scot ?
That wise old saw hast thou forgot,
" That he who suppers wi' the Deil,
Lang spoon maun hae to sup his kail!" '
Here, Jockie, I my temper lost,
I'd hae my say whate'er the cost.
' D—-n you,' says I, ' you ca' yoursel' the Deil,
You are na blate my bonnie chiel.
The Deil's a saunt compared wi' you,
You yelley-livered, bandy-leggèd Jew ;
Quack doctor, purse-proud swaggerin' Jack,
I'faith I'll lay you on your back.'

He listened, looked, and gravely smiled
To hear his Majesty reviled
By simple clay so easily beguiled.

Thoughtful he stood, and stroked his beard.
Then, Presto, vanished—disappeared !

Gone like a flash, I looked and wondered,
And as I gaped and gazed and pondered,
Beneath my feet the ground began to tremble,
With earthquake shock to rock and rumble ;
And o'er the scene thick darkness crept,
Deep gloom prevailed, the soft wind slept,
Then lightning flared with vivid sheen,
Blinding and dazzling my bewildered een !
And thunder bellowed forth with awful roar,
Echoing from shore to sea, from sea to shore.
From Lucklaw to Drumcarrow, from Drumcarrow
      to Kinkell,
Roaring and rattling with resounding swell,
Peal followed peal, and flash on flash,
Hissing and rumbling with terrific crash ;
The wind subdued burst forth anew,
And howling, whistling, wilder blew ;
Deep groans and wailing filled the air,
Of souls in anguish and despair !
Loud shouts of ' fore,' and clash of cleeks,
And demon golfers' yells and shrieks,
Commingling with the mournful wail
Of sea-birds swept before the gale !

At last the thunder ceased and all was still,
Deep silence reigned o'er dale and hill ;
Then forth a lurid radiance glowed,
Fan-like from earth to heaven it flowed,
Deep ruby red, the hue of blood,
And in the midst an awful presence stood—-
Majestic, pale, towering in aspect grand,
Hell's chieftain, prince of the rebel band,
Who fell defying Heaven's command.
O'er lofty brow tossed his dishevelled hair,
A front deep lined with thought and care,
And eyes with shaggy eyebrows pent,
Which fierceness to their glances lent ;
Those eyes which blazed with hate and sadness,
Strangers alike to hope, to love, and gladness.
With lips of scorn, whence insults leap,
And lies and calumnies and curses deep ;
Scoffings, revilings, blasphemies malign
Against Omnipotence and laws divine !

With awe and terror struck, I trembling gazed,
Spell-bound, bewildered, and amazed
To think that I should hap to contemplate
The lineaments of H—l's great potentate !
With shuddering dread, I feared his eagle eye
Should wretch like me by cruel chance espy.

D

Alas, my fate!   The hated glance it fell,
Nought could escape the blighting eye of H—l;
Staggering, I fell like riven oak
Struck to the earth by lightning stroke!

Jockie, my lad, I swooned away;
Of sense bereft, how long, I cannot say.
Hard by where old Daa drives his trade
O' ginger-beer and leemonade.
I felt the cool, soft morning air
To fan my cheek and raise my hair;
Conscious at last, I raised my eyes,
Conceive my horror and surprise,
To see friend Clootie stand before me,
Leering and grinning, bending o'er me!
My heart was well-nigh like to burst
With fear and hatred and disgust.
I cried, besceched him to forgive me,
And begged him on my knees to leave me.
He laughed, and told me hold my jargon,
To stir my stumps, make good my bargain.
' The match you know,' he said, ' ain't ended,
And luck may turn, and mine be mended,
The remaining holes may fall to me,
Then Skipper dear, where will you be?
I've not had one, and eight you've taken,

You need one more to save your bacon—
One little hole, to save your soul!
I stand to lose name, fame, and purse,
Not that I care a tinker's curse ;
But you, should fortune now forsake you,
Your freedom gone, my slave I make you.
Play up, and man-like save your skin,
Strike for your name and native green.'

I heard, and as I gazed upon him,
Transformed he seemed, some change come o'er him ;
He caught my eye, divined my thought,
And gave the explanation sought.—
' To honour you I've changed my suit,
My taste and style none can dispute ;
I now assume my sporting dress,
The garb I wear when I mean business ;
I've donned my tail, and doffed my boots,
You see me in my native cloots.'
Man's fond, familiar, friendly devil
Aye gracious, debonair and civil ;
Smiling he stood, his arms akimbo,
The Deil himself, the Prince o' Limbo.

Oh, Jockie, crushed wi' grief and shame,
A prey to fear, remorse and blame,

Like vessel storm-stressed in the bay,
Her rudder gone, her masts away ;
Left to the mercy of the waves, and tossed
A helpless hulk and well-nigh lost.
Belief in succour still remained,
The distant life-boat hope sustained.
So, stranded in this awful hole,
I turned to Heaven to save my soul.
I prayed, beseeched the powers on high,
To help me in my agony.
I prayed, as ne'er I prayed before ;
In anguish keen I vowed and swore,
This trouble gone, this sorrow ended,
My wicked life should be amended ;
This struggle o'er, this combat passed,
This drucken bout should be my last.
Then hope, sweet hope, began to flow,
And swell my breast with genial glow ;
Self-trust and courage that had gane
Wi' fiery rush, cam' back again.
My native pride, love o' the game,
Blazed in my heart like altar flame.
I felt that tho' a fool I'd been,
I still could battle for the green.
Resolved, restored, I rose defiant,
O'er doubts and fears I sprang triumphant.

'Clootie,' says I, as cool and cheeky
As lawyer lad frae gude Auld Reekie,
'I'm willin' to resume the game,
A stroke a hole, and terms the same.
But had I kent what I ken noo,
And sober been, instead o' fou,
I'd seen you fried in your ain brimstane
Ere I had linked to sic a bargain.
A bargain ca' it, wi' changed condections
That won't admit of definections.
The man I bargained wi', in boots,
Is now a beast wi' tail and cloots,
And——'

'Confound your check, you old transgressor,
You phrase and jaw like a Professor.
Enough of all this d—d palaver,
Your blasted bletherin' and haver.
My tail, it is a thing of beauty,
By Jove, you'll find it do its duty.
Between us you will see such golf,
Ere long you'll cry " I've had enough."
Then tee your ball, resume your game,
Strike off once more for purse and fame.'

But Skipper, pause and kindly tell us
About that tail, it is so curious.

Why, Jock, the thocht o't gars me scunner,
With it he dealt me sic dishonour.
Albeit, it was indeed a stunner,
I canna think o't without wunner.
It was at least a fathom lang,
And tapered, at the end a stang
Like harpoon dart or arrow head,
Glittering and gleaming fiery red.
'Twas nae doot gey thick at the root,
But that was covered by his coat.
So soople, he could gi'e a skelp wi't,
Could licht his pipe, or pick his teeth wi't ;
And at his pleasure, short or lang,
It telescoped up to the stang.
Besides it was a choice dumb caddie,
And quite as helpful as a laddie,
By his left side he made it swirl
Around his clubs, like snake to twirl.
They stood erect quite near and handy
As 'neath the arm o' Jock or Sandy.
To see him like a puddock squattin',
His tail stiff oot, the sod pat, pattin',
Viewing his putt to find the line,
'Twas enough to mak' a cuddy grin.
There was little grin in me that mornin',
I wasna in a mood for scornin'.

The game I was about to witness,
It wasna in my power to compass.
My fears they soon were realised,
And my poor play that I so prized
I saw eclipsed and beaten hollow—
A bitter pill for me to swallow.
Hole after hole he stole away,
With masterly and brilliant play.
And ever and anon he jeered me,
And with his cursed tail he skeered me.
That tail! It curled and squirmed and gleamed,
The stang it glowed, red-hot it seemed;
Whate'er it touched it brunt and bristled,
The very sod it scorched and frizzled.

I played my best, I strove and swat;
Wha could contend 'gainst foe like that?
A stroke a hole, what use to me
Against a Deil who averaged three?

Gude three-score years I'd kent the green,
And many a gallant match I'd seen,
Lang, lang before I was a caddie,
When golfin' daft a fisher laddie.
Wi' keen delight I still remember
The glorious gatherin's o' September,

When eager golfers came to seek,
And share the joys o' ' Medal Week.'
They mustered strong, a manly band.
The wale o' gentry o' the land ;
Among them golfers known to fame,
Old hands, scratch players o' the game,
The Woods, Sir Hope, the gallant Grant ;
That swiper grand, R. Oliphant ;
Pattullo, Stirling, Messieux, Condie,
Holcroft, Playfair, Haig, and Fairlie ;
Sir David Baird, Sir Ralph Anstruther,
All players stout, and many another ;
Forby of course, a wheen o' duffers,
Second fiddles, middlin' golfers,
Most worthy men, but poor performers,
Like Mr Patton, Puddle Mudie,
Or cheery Small, the laird o' Foodie ;
The rattlin' red-nosed Craigie Halket ;
Flash Jim, the swell, for slang and racket ;
Clanranald, spruce, the tartan dandy,
And, ' dem it,' sweet as sugar candy ;
Mount Melville's laird, aye debonair,
True gentleman beyond compare ;
Dundas, Gillespie, Wemyss, and Craigie,
Pitarro's bard, the wag Carnegie,
And stalwart Saddle, big and burly,

Tho' grim his look, he ne'er was surly,
'Twas he that swore or e'en pretended
That nature's laws were clean suspended
(Save us, mortals, sic a shame!)
To 'spite and spoil *his* little game!!'
Of handsome men a grand display,
As rarely seen on Summer's day.
Kilgraston's sons, Sir Frank the chief,
Falkland, Charlton, and Moncrieff;
And mony mair o' birth and name
That came to view the Royal game.
Blythe Allan then was in his prime,
The finest player o' his time.
Tom Morris, too, a lad of twenty,
Ere long renowned for honours plenty,
Good player still, an honest man,
As ever lifted club in han',
Long may he live the green to guard,
And at his pleasure sand the sward,
And when at last 'neath sod he's landed.
Wi' blessings may his grave be sanded.
And ither lads, professionals o' mark,
Kirks, Straths, and Pirie, Herds, and Park;
Besides a lot I canna' mind,
All clever players o' their kind.

But ne'er a one a club could handle,
Play sic a game, or haud the candle,
To that auld limb o' sin, the rip,
Who had me in his ugly grip.

Frae the 'Hole Across' in 'Hell' he landed,
That I foresaw it was intended.
As I gaed by I heard him laughin',
And with the little deils a-daffin'.
I fondly hoped he'd come to grief,
And with hole or half I'd get relief;
But no such luck, alas for me,
For again he nailed the hole in three!
The next three holes he did in seven,
And, Heaven preserve me, we were even!
My eight holes gane, the game a' square,
Oh, Jock, I shuddered in despair.

What skill o' mortal could prevail
Against a foe wi' cloots and tail!
The tail it now was blazin' red,
And from the point bright sparks it shed,
And squirmed and curled as if wi' glee,
Possessed wi' joy at leatherin' me.
Tremblin', abashed, depressed, I stood;
My threatened fate, it chilled my blood,

Cold swat bedewed me, froze my marrow,
I felt like puddock 'neath a harrow,
Or thief that views the rope a danglin'
Prepared and ready for his stranglin'.

The morning breeze blew cool and free,
Sweet, fresh, and caller frae the sea ;
The sun, with ruddy cheek, had risen
Not long from forth his watery prison ;
The strand was bathed with golden light,
And all was beautiful and bright.
As for auld Sin, he stood serene,
He little cared to view the scene.
His arms were crossed, one hand on chin,
And on his face sardonic grin.
With keen and glittering eye he viewed me,
And seemed to look right thro' and thro' me,
My poor heart throbbing with affright,
Full well he gauged my sorry plight.

'Skipper,' quoth he, 'how dost thou feel ?
You've had your tussle with the Deil ;
Hast got a lesson, eh, in Golf ?
Just one hole more and then—enough !
I've seen your swagger, heard your boast,
Methinks I've got you now—on toast.'
Oh, Jock, so horrible his smile,

Just like a loathsome crocodile,
Wi' sea-green een, and dreadfu' snigger,
About to supper on a nigger!

Cool and composed I tried to look,
As calm as might an aged rook
On tree top perched, or giddy mast
Exposed to wild and stormy blast;
But still a shadowy hope remained
By my late fervent vow sustained,
That should the powers aboon preserve me,
Good play or fickle fortune save me,
To mend my life I would endeavour,
And cursed drink forswear for ever.

· Satan, you say, I'm yours to roast;
But you prefer me served on toast,
Like a fat kidney fried wi' bacon,
You'll find me teugh or I'm mistaken.
The honour's great, the compliment I feel,
To be a chosen tit-bit for the Deil.
But michty strange it seems to be,
Sic honour should be kept for me,
When you might have made selection
From swells and sinners o' distinction :
Ginerals, Cornels, and sodger gentry ;
Gude kens! there's wale o' them and plenty!

'Mong Clairgy, Lawyers, and Professors,
Poor folk in trade, and sma' transgressors.
Save us man ! You micht hae grippet
A Provost wi' an ermine tippet,
Or eke a consequential Bailie,
Or Councillor fu' wise and wily.
Instead, to nab a poor auld caddie,
'Twas *mean*,' I tell't him, Jock Pitbladdie.
' Cocksure you hae me in your grip—
There's mony a slip 'tween cup and lip.
Eneugh ! I'm weary and half dead.
Lost or saved, I maun win hame to bed.'
At my free speech old Sooty growled,
And at me glared malevolent and scowled ;
Then tee'd wi' care, his ball addressed,
And stood a golfer grand confessed.

Oh, Jock, I think I see him yet ;
That scene I never can forget,
Broad-shouthered, slight o' powerful bield,
Long-armed, lean-shankit, strapping chield ;
His fearfu' tail, red, stiff, and stark,
And at the end the gleamin' spark !
Gudesake, to think the Prince o' H—l,
At oor grand game should bear the bell !
He drove a long, low ripping shot,

O'er brig and road to the green he got.
I followed true, for me right good,
But, alas, I landed on the road!
My heart it sank, but I lay clean,
For muckle waur I might hae been.
I took my cleek—Oh, blessed happy lick!
Home went the ball fornent the stick,
Dead as a corp, or Julius Cæsar,
Baalam's ass, or Nebuchenezzar.
Forward I ran, richt eager, to the green
To see how good my luck had been.
Fortune indeed had smiled upon me,
I lay a dead and perfect stymie!
Auld Sin he looked as black as thunder
To be so foiled, I dinna wonder.
I sprang wi' glee, and gied a howl,—
' I've stymed the Deil and saved my sowl!'
' Villain!' he roared, ' You sot, you've done me,
My malison and curse be on ye!'
With that he struck me wi' his tail
Right on the stern, just like a flail,
So cruel, strong, severe a lounder,
In faith it felled me flat's a flounder.

I ken nae mair, all was confusion,
How long I lay I have nae notion.

My friends they tell me I was found
Senseless, and dead-like, on the ground ;
Home to my bed they kindly bore me,
Made fruitless efforts to restore me,
But all in vain, for fever seized me,
And friendly death well-nigh released me.
Seven days and nights I raved and tossed,
For ever screaming lost, lost, lost !
The ravings of a fevered brain,
As I went o'er and o'er again
The scenes and horrors of that night,
Freezing my listeners with affright.
A weary time ; but, to be brief,
Kind Heaven in mercy sent relief.
At last, far gane, I found my head,
And kent the folk about my bed ;
Among them I was pleased to view
My worthy friend Nurse Killiegrew,
For she had with her presence blessed me,
And thro' my illness watched and nursed me.

I had their warm congratulations,
And their demands for explanations
About my ravings wild and furious
(Women are aye sae keen and curious).
' Poor man,' quoth Nurse, ' you've had a lesson,

'Twill ease your mind to mak' confession.'
Abashed, ashamed, I hesitated,
At last, with pain, my tale related.

My yarn, of course, made great sensation ;
They groaned and grat at the narration,
Save Nurse, who shook her head in sadness,
Incredulous, declared my story madness.
Said she, ' You fancy you have seen the Deevil,
And golfed and bargained wi' the Prince o' Evil ;
You've had the horrors, it would seem,
And what you tell us was a drunkard's dream.'

' Pardon,' said I,—I felt quite nettled,—
' I do not think you've fairly settled
The nature of my strange distraction,
At least not to my simple satisfaction.
To clear myself, my honour tells me,
A stern necessity compels me,
Against your most injurious explanations
I have strong proof in bodily sensations.
For obvious reasons, I would fain refrain
From reference to the region of my pain.
The cause I've in my story tell't ye,
The skelp wi' tail Auld Hooky dealt me ;
Further, my breeks, or I'm mistaen,

Will furnish proof both strong and plain.
Bring forth the breeks ; as sure as leeks is leeks
You'll find the proof upon the breeks.'
The breeks they brought, o' good grey tweed,
And laid them oot upon the bed.
It was indeed a solemn moment,
Mysel', six worthy women present,—
A wise, discreet, respectable sederunt.
Auld Meg Kilgour, a clever howdie ;
That virtuous woman, Jenny Braidie,
As dink and braw as ony lady ;
The aged clack wife, Nelly Gourlay ;
Good Jeanie Tosh, and stout Bell Lonie :
And last, the wisest o' the crew,
My worthy nurse, Miss Killiegrew.

The carlines they put on their specs,
Six pair o' een bore on the breeks ;
Awe-struck they saw upon the seat,
Brunt black and deep, the mark complete
Of Clootie's tail, like the broad arrow,
Clear and distinct as tooth o' harrow !

The sicht o't caused great consternation,
Hech sirs ! Gudesake ! and sic-like exclamation.

F

Jean Tosh she gat as white's a sheet ;
And Nell and Bell began to greet,
But Meg had nae sic trepidation,
And wanted mair investigation.
' Cummers,' says she, ' let's see his sark,
Aiblins it likewise bears the mark.'
' Fie !' Jenny cried, wi' blushing cheeks,
' Eneugh ! we've seen the Skipper's breeks,
Sic zeal may weel become a howdie,
I draw the line at breeks,' quo' Jenny Braidie.
' What !' Meg rejoined, ' you pented jade,
You dare to scorn my honest trade !
'Tis ill for you to mak' reflection,
Your ain will scarcely stand inspection.'
And snorting red, on mischief bent,
She turned to me for my consent.
I saw that things were getting serious,
And feared they jauds so keen and curious.
Meg's birse was up and no mistake,
Her match she had in Jean the rake.
'Twas time to still the wordy clatter,
And pour the ile on troubled water.
' Leddies,' said I, ' your sympathy is precious,
To me you've been most kind and gracious,
With all your care I'm deeply gratified,
And as to proof, completely satisfied.'

Nurse heard me, saw the cummer's zeal,
And looked as if diverted weel.
She laughed, amused at the sensation,
But flat refused the explanation,
And chaffed and scoffed in huge derision,
Declaring they had lost their reason.
' You doited women, don't you see
What is so evident,' says she,
' This good-for-nothing drunken wight
Has sat upon his pipe alight,
No doubt the cause of mark and pain.
To me it is as porridge plain.'

' Nurse!' I exclaimed, enraged, indignant,
' Your explanation is repugnant
To reason, sense, and proof, and feelin';
Don't think that with a fool you're dealin',
For though to drink a slave I've been,
I say it, with contrition keen,
I ne'er had horrors, what they ca' *D. T.*
In Latin tongue, whatever that may be ;
You haud your ain, and I keep my opinion,
I ken my failin's, I'm but human.'
('Twas nae use arguing wi' a woman.)

Now Jock my story's told, my yarn is ended,
Some things there be that can't be mended ;

As broken hearts, and damaged reputation,
Like club-heid gane past reparation,
Beyond the savin' powers o' glue,
New leather face, or nails, or screw.
Not so, thank God, an evil habit,
Heaven spare me that I live to prove it.
I've tottered on destruction's brink,
Have wallowed in the slough o' drink,
Have good despised and lived for evil,
And golfed and bargained wi' the Deevil.
Thank goodness, that's all gone and changed,
By other hands my life's arranged.
I'm like the chield in Bunyan's story,
That pilgrim on his road to glory,
Sair hudden doon wi' muckle sack
Chokefu' o' sins upon his back,
Warstlin' and pechin' on his weary way,
The burden heavier growin' every day.
Heaven heard his prayer, the burden fell,
And rolled behind him to the jaws o' H—l.
Joyous and free, gone all his sadness,
Grateful he sang, and danced in gladness.
I, grim auld pilgrim, in like manner,
Compared wi' him a hardened sinner,
Thro' forty years I've burden borne,
By self despised, of men the scorn.

Now, safe forever from the curse
That starved my body, toomed my purse,
I've anchored in a peacefu' haven,
No more for drink the cruel cravin'.
No more the ' Public' haunts for me,
The drunkard's shout, the maddening glee,
The ribald jokes, and songs, and laughter,
The sickening pangs that follow after.
Gone, gone forever, all the filth and folly,
The aches, the woes, the melancholy ;
I've cast the old, put on the new,
Three cheers then for the ribbon blue,
And blessings on Nurse Killiegrew !